That Darn Cat

by THE GORDONS

A story adapted from the Walt Disney production THAT DARN CAT based upon the book entitled UNDERCOVER CAT by The Gordons.

SCHOLASTIC BOOK SERVICES

NEW YORK • TORONTO • LONDON • AUCKLAND • SYDNEY • TOKYO

Copyright © 1965 by Walt Disney Productions. World rights reserved. Adapted from the Walt Disney film THAT DARN CAT, based upon the book entitled UNDERCOVER CAT by the Gordons, published by Doubleday & Company, Inc., copyright © 1963 by Mildred Gordon and Gordon Gordon. This edition is published by Scholastic Book Services, a division of Scholastic Magazines, Inc., by arrangement with Walt Disney Productions and Doubleday & Company.

1st printing . . . . December 1973

Printed in the U. S. A.

That Darn Cat

D.C. (Darn Cat) Randall left the house every night at nine to make his regular rounds.

D. C. Randall heard the cuckoo clock in the hall strike nine and knew he should get up. He could tell without opening his eyes that it was a lovely evening. The air was crisp with a hint of spring. And through the open bedroom window came the scent of orange blossoms — orange blossoms and the delectable odor of fish cooking.

Suddenly, he sat bolt upright. There would be a beautiful silvery salmon in the window of the delicatessen down the street and Mr. Meyer, the proprietor, would give him some. Sitting on the edge of the bed, he slowly washed his face. First he wiped the sleep from his eyes, then scrubbed behind his ears. Next, he shook himself vigorously till his shiny black and blond hair lay neatly in place. Then he jumped down off the bed and left the house through a small opening in the kitchen door.

D. C. (short for Darn Cat) Randall was a large,

worldly-wise Siamese. Humans, he believed, were for the most part a rather stupid, predictable lot, and any cat with average intelligence could train them to do his bidding in short order. But he was sentimental about his humans, the Randall family. Actually, the capricious, romantic teenager Patti was his girl and he adored her. Of course he was also fond of Ingrid, who was older, and of Mr. and Mrs. Randall.

D. C. paused on the doorstep to plan his evening. He would wind up at the delicatessen but *en route* he would make several stops, for, like most cats, he was a natural-born moocher and had a regular route worked out. He had many friends all over the neighborhood. The Joneses, for instance, were always good for a bit of fresh liver. The Travis family was strong on steak, and the Krauches were hamburger people. When he felt the need of a good solid meal he always stopped at Sam's Diner. He needed only

He was a steady customer at Sam's lunch counter.

Garbage cans held a great fascination for him.

to hop up on a stool and the "blue-plate special" would invariably be set before him. Too, he always got vicarious fun out of doing the alleys, rummaging through boxes and garbage cans in the manner of any ordinary cat, although actually he was of royal Siamese lineage.

When he finally reached the delicatessen, Mr. Meyer was wrapping up the salmon for a customer. Another two minutes and D. C. would have been too late. It was beyond a doubt the most devastatingly aromatic salmon D. C. had ever smelled, and D. C. was an authority on salmon. He knew instantly that he must have a sizable chunk of that salmon even if he had to give up one of his nine lives.

Next to his home, Darn Cat's favorite place was the delicatessen, where the salmon was delicious.

As the customer left the store with the large package of fish, D. C. padded along behind him. Finally the man turned into a rather shabby apartment house and climbed a flight of back stairs. To D. C.'s frustration, he quickly stepped inside and closed the door.

Margaret Miller sat bound and gagged in the living room. She heard one of her captors, Dan, open the kitchen door and the man called Iggy come in. As she listened intently, she told herself she must be having a bad dream. Only a few hours ago she had been at the bank as usual at her teller's window.

"Everything go okay?" she heard Dan ask. And then, "Let's see the papers."

"Just look at 'em," Iggy was boasting. "We made page one all over — every paper, except for one miserable rag that puts us on page four."

They came into the living room bringing the

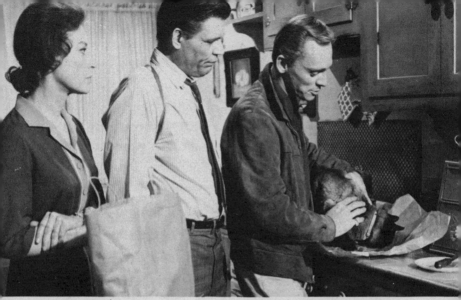

Naturally D.C. did not know he was in the home of bank robbers who were holding Margaret captive.

papers with them. Dan read aloud: "Bank robbers stage daring daylight holdup. Two armed men, wearing Halloween masks, robbed the North Valley Bank early today, seizing a teller, Margaret Miller, 45, to shield their getaway. They escaped with an estimated $250,000.'"

Iggy's eyes glittered as he dug his fingers into the suitcase of money which lay open on a table. "How about her?" he asked, nodding toward Margaret. "We have to do something with her."

"I don't know," Dan said. He took off the gag and Margaret moved her jaws painfully. "We're stuck with you," he said, as he untied her, "so you can take over the cooking. As long as you behave

9

yourself and don't get any ideas, you won't get hurt. Understand?"

Before she could speak, the kitchen door rattled loudly as though someone was trying to get in. Iggy held his gun on Margaret while Dan went to investigate. Cautiously he unlatched the door, gun leveled, and looked out. There was no one about.

Suddenly Dan felt a movement about his ankles and he jumped back, startled. It was D. C. He went straight for the salmon which lay on the kitchen table.

"Come on in, both of you," Dan called to Iggy. "You and your fish!" he added disgustedly.

D. C. put his forepaws on the table and inhaled. "How about a nice hunk of fish?" Iggy asked him, grinning.

"Get that flea-bag cat out of here," Dan told him.

"Aw, I like cats," Iggy said, cutting off a piece of the fish. D. C. jumped up on the table and began eating hungrily.

The men turned to the living room, and as Margaret watched Darn Cat eating, some of the terror ran out of her. She stroked D. C. thoughtfully. He was only a cat, but he didn't hate anyone, he didn't hold a gun on her, and he would be her friend if invited.

Tears of frustration came to her eyes. Here was her one link to the outside world and it was mute. As she petted him, her fingers found the collar about his neck. If she could only write a message and somehow fasten it to the collar. But she had no pencil, nothing. Suddenly an idea struck her.

Standing with her back to the doorway, so that the criminals could not see what she was doing, she quickly removed the collar. D. C. was so busy eating he did not object. She pulled off her wristwatch, which luckily had an expansion bracelet. Hastily she started to scratch "HELP" on the back of the watch. Before she had finished she panicked and slipped the watch over D. C.'s head.

In a desperate move, she grabbed the surprised cat, ran to the door, and tossed him out. This

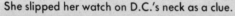

She slipped her watch on D.C.'s neck as a clue.

brought Iggy and Dan on the run, guns leveled. Margaret leaned her trembling body against the closed door for support.

"One more move like that," Dan told her, "and it will be your last."

"I didn't try to make a break, did I?" she retorted. "The cat wanted out, that's all."

Margaret saw the anger in Dan's face and it frightened her as much as the gun.

D. C. sat on the upper landing and meditated upon the eccentricities of human behavior. He'd been up on the table, eating, minding his own business, and suddenly this woman steals his collar, puts this infernal ticking thing around his neck and throws him out.

First, he must get the contraption off. He shook his head, he raked the watch against the stair railing, he tried backing out of it (though he knew that was foolish), and he attempted to kick it off with his hind foot. He succeeded only in getting a crick in his leg. He went home, hoping one of his humans would help him. A steady tick like that, right in the ear, could drive a cat mad.

His girl, Patti, and her boyfriend, Canoe Henderson, were in the living room watching television. Canoe, so called because of his enormous, awkward feet, was the boy next door, and to the romantic

"Don't dribble that mile-high sandwich all over the carpet," Patti Randall told her friend Canoe.

Patti, he would always be just that. They had grown up together and Canoe enjoyed family status. D. C. approved of Canoe because he was always building many-layered sandwiches. The bits of food that fell out were delicious.

Canoe was stretched out on the floor, watching the news. D. C. nudged him but Canoe didn't notice the watch. Instead he gave D. C. a bit of his sandwich.

Suddenly Patti pointed at the screen. "Look! That's Miss Miller!" she cried. "You know — at our bank!"

They listened breathlessly to the newscaster's account of the holdup in their neighborhood, then

Patti excused herself to do her homework. Canoe watched till the newscast ended, idly rubbing D.C.'s ears. He happened to glance down and see the watch.

"Eleven-fifteen!" he exclaimed. "Ye gods, I've got to get my sleep." He stuffed the last of the sandwich in his mouth and left. D. C. went out with him, rather disgusted.

At that moment D. C.'s other girl, Ingrid, drove up with a character from down the street whom they called Gregory. D. C. had little respect for Gregory, and even less for his big, fat, stupid bulldog, Blitzy. He told Ingrid all about the thing on his neck in his best loud baritone voice, but it was hopeless. She would pay no attention to him as long as that Gregory was with her. Well, he thought, I'll fix his wagon. And he took off down the street.

At the front door, Gregory was saying, "It's a

"I bagged a Gadwall duck," Gregory told Ingrid.

date, then?" Ingrid nodded and Gregory continued, "Mother cooks the world's best duck. About eight tomorrow night?"

"I adore roast duck," Ingrid said. "See you in the morning."

Gregory said good night and started home, humming.

D. C. had arrived there ahead of him. His route led through a petunia bed, across a manicured lawn, around a cage of uneasy pigeons, and to the back screen door.

As usual, Blitzy was on the job. The kitchen window leading to the service porch was slightly ajar, and Blitzy reacted with such fury that he almost strangled on his own barking. D. C. jiggled the screen door with the skill of a safecracker. He ignored the dog, which was the worst possible insult to a proud defender of life and property like Blitzy.

Not even his wildest anticipations had prepared D. C. for the sight he saw on the porch. From a beam in the ceiling hung the most beautiful duck he had ever seen. It required considerable maneuvering, and great skill, but D. C. finally snared it. Blitzy, on the verge of an asthmatic convulsion, made such a ruckus that neither heard the approach of Gregory's car.

Success came not a second too soon to D. C. At the very moment that Gregory came running to the

When D.C. stole the duck, Gregory gave chase. But he tripped over a low hedge and fell headlong.

back door, alarmed at Blitzy's barking, D. C. lunged out with the duck in his mouth. Gregory followed in hot pursuit.

Darn Cat found the plump duck a great handicap to his speed and it is difficult to say what would have happened had Gregory not tripped over a low ornamental fence, and fallen into the petunia bed. D.C. gazed upon his prostrate form with deep satisfaction, took another good hold on the duck, and dashed off.

By the time Gregory was able to get up, D. C. was no longer in sight. Outraged, Gregory went charging down the street to the Randall home and battered at the door. Then he put his finger on the bell and left it there until a sleepy-eyed Patti in robe and slippers opened the door.

"That darn cat of yours stole my duck," he began without bothering to greet her. "I've had just about all I can take too. I spent all day in a duck blind, in the soaking rain. Nearly caught pneumonia. And I get one single, beautiful Gadwall duck. And that flea-ridden fiend has to go steal it!"

Now *Patti* was angry. "And I suppose he reached up, unlatched the screen, opened the door, and walked in?"

"He walked in all right. That cat could walk into Fort Knox."

"Well, that does it," Patti said, furious. "Of all the preposterous, unfair, monstrous accusations — "

She stopped suddenly as D. C. padded in, walking very proudly, head held high, bearing the duck in his mouth. She flashed a guilty look at Gregory, and grabbed at the duck, but D. C. fastened a death hold on it. They wrestled, and then Patti gave a hard wrench and tore it from his mouth, shredding the duck somewhat in the process.

"Serves you right," she snapped, handing Gregory the duck just as one of its legs came off in her hand. "What do you expect a cat to do if you leave your game where he can get it? He's a hunter, like you."

"He's a thief," Gregory said, staring down in

D.C. knew that his girl would finally notice the contraption on his neck and take it off.

hatred at D. C. "And if I catch him on my property once more, he's going to get a pants-full of buck-shot. Nine times if I have to."

"Gregory Benson, if you dare—"

But Gregory wasn't listening. He stalked away with his prize Gadwall, much the worse for wear, under his arm.

Patti bent down to try to console D. C. and dis-covered the watch. She yanked it off and went screaming to Ingrid's room.

"It's a wristwatch! It's running!" she told the startled, sleepy Ingrid. "D. C. was wearing it!"

Ingrid yawned. "Now what do you suppose that clever, innocent cat will bring home next? Let's hope it will be the Hope diamond."

"Look," the excited Patti continued. "There are letters on the back. H—E—L—. Do you suppose someone tried to scratch 'HELP'?"

"Patti, you are absolutely hopeless. Now stop imagining wild stories and go to bed."

"But don't you think we ought to call the police? Maybe some woman's in danger — say, it could be poor Miss Miller. I heard over TV a while ago..."

Ingrid interrupted. "Patti, I absolutely forbid you to go to the police with one of your romantic dreams. Understand?"

"Check," Patti replied meekly. But she went to her room smiling to herself. D. C. was having his usual bedtime saucer of milk on her bed. "I wouldn't dream of going to the police," she told him. "This is a case for the FBI."

Patti showed the watch to her sister. "What will that clever cat bring home next?" Ingrid asked.

Patti was so awed when she walked into the sacred precincts of the FBI the next morning that her courage almost failed her. And it probably would have, had not a young agent named Zeke Kelso been so nice to her.

He listened to her unusual story with growing interest and when she showed him the wristwatch she could tell that he was quite excited.

Patti thought he had the nicest smile. "I don't know," he said, shaking his head. "In all the history of the FBI we've never had a cat as an informant."

He excused himself to consult his superior. Supervisor Newton agreed that although they had no proof that the watch was Margaret Miller's, still

Patti went to the FBI and told the unusual story to a handsome young agent named Zeke Kelso.

they did not dare discard the possibility. The criminals had seemingly vanished into thin air and so far the FBI had no lead.

Patti was very proud when Zeke brought her home in a Bureau car. It had been decided that he would set up operations at the Randall home and attempt to follow D. C. on his nightly rounds, in the hope that he would return to the house where he got the watch. As Zeke was getting his suitcase of equipment, Patti glanced out of the corner of her eye at the house next door. The drapes were parted a slit and an eye was peering out.

"Oh, oh," she whispered. "Don't look now, but Mrs. MacDougall is watching as usual. She's a human radar system. Knows everything that goes on in the neighborhood. Mom and Dad are on their vacation, you know, but Mom says she doesn't worry a bit about us with Mrs. MacDougall on the job."

Zeke groaned. The success of his plans depended upon complete secrecy. "Mrs. MacDougall is always scolding her poor husband," Patti continued, "and he's pretty cantankerous. He's hard of hearing but Dad says that's a blessing. When he gets fed up he just yanks out his hearing aid."

Patti showed Zeke to Ingrid's room in the rear of the house. "I think my sister's room will be the best. It's farthest from the action, and there's quite a bit

"Come on out from under the bed, D.C.," Patti coaxed. "You are now an informant for the FBI."

of action around this house — normally, that is. And you can see when D. C. leaves through his private entrance in the back door."

In the dead center of the bed stretched D. C. He was making funny noises and his legs were twitching. "He's chasing something in his sleep," Patti interpreted.

Agent Kelso gazed in disbelief. "That is a cat?" It was the most formidable feline he had ever seen.

Patti put a hand on D. C.'s shoulder and shook him gently. "Hey, you lazy thing, wake up. This is your FBI agent!"

Slowly Darn Cat eased one eye open. He was annoyed that his girl would awaken him in the middle of the day when she knew he needed his sleep. His eye moved to Zeke, and he wondered who the man was. He had never seen him before and if he never saw him again it would be too soon. D.C. closed the eye. Sometimes the humans went away if he pretended they weren't there.

At a strange sound, almost like hissing, D. C. rose to flight position. Patti reassured him, however, and he realized it was only the man sneezing.

"Sorry," Zeke said. "I'm allergic to cat fur." He sneezed again and tears welled up in his eyes. He unpacked his equipment and put it on a small table which Patti provided. Besides a compact sending and receiving set, there was a camera and a fingerprinting kit.

As he admitted later, Zeke made his first big mistake when he took D. C.'s picture. When the flash went off, Darn Cat disappeared under the bed and refused to come out. He appeared to be in a very angry and uncooperative mood. If a dangerous killer had been lying in wait, Zeke would have known what to do. But he had had no experience with cats. He suspected that if he attempted to pull D. C. out he might lose a hand.

"When I count three," Patti said, "grab!"

On three, they both lunged. D. C. lashed out at his assailant with the speed of a Samoan knife thrower. Zeke missed capturing him, possibly because of the blood running down his hand, but Patti got a hammer hold on D. C.'s hind leg.

"Now I've got to fingerprint — I mean pawprint

"I've got to fingerprint — I mean pawprint him," Zeke said, "since he will be working for us."

him," Zeke said resolutely, after Patti had bandaged his scratched hand.

"Do you *have* to? He's getting awfully mad."

Zeke nodded. "It's required. First thing we always do with an informant. Besides, we might pick up his trail from last night if he stepped in the mud or something."

It was agreed that the bathroom was the best place to attempt the job. Patti put D. C. beside the washbasin, and over his loud protests, kept him pinned down. Zeke studied the fingerprint card, which had squares for each of the ten human fingers. "Let's see," he murmured, "shall I put it in the square for the thumb or for one of the fingers?"

"Hurry up," Patti warned. "He's getting suspicious."

Zeke squinted through reddened, swollen eyes. He grabbed a forepaw and inked it thoroughly. Then the doorbell sounded.

"Canoe!" Patti exclaimed. "He's the boy next door."

Zeke looked up, startled. "Get rid of him as fast as you can. And for goodness sake, hurry back here."

It seemed to him that Patti was gone for hours. D.C. struggled, lurched, and swatted at Zeke. In fact, he put his paws every place except on the fingerprint chart. Just when Zeke thought he had him, he felt the teeth sinking in. Zeke let out a great cry and D. C. escaped. In a streak, he climbed up the

D.C. put his paws every place except on the chart, so Zeke took a perfect print off his own face.

shower curtain and jumped onto a high windowsill. He opened the screen with one swish of his paw and was gone.

When Patti returned, she saw the blank fingerprint card. "You didn't get it?" she asked.

Zeke looked at himself in the mirror and grinned triumphantly. He took a tape from his kit and removed one of the many black pawprints from his face. Looking at it, he said, "Perfect. Absolutely perfect."

A few hours later, at the FBI field office, Zeke Kelso found himself conducting a briefing session unique in the annals of the Federal Bureau of Investigation.

"This is a photo of the informant," Zeke told the other agents. "Blue eyes, black and tan hair — "

"This is a photograph of the informant," he said, holding up a huge enlargement of the picture he had taken earlier. When the group of agents assigned to the case saw what they were to follow, there was great consternation. How do you trail a cat? they wanted to know.

"They go through fences and under culverts," one agent objected. "They climb trees and telephone poles too."

Zeke nodded, and suppressed a grin. "This is the way we'll handle the surveillance," he began. "When the informant leaves the house, our job will be to tail him loosely. It's important that he does not know we're following him. It might disturb his pattern. I will be at the control center in a back room of the Randall house. You will keep in touch with me at all times and report your exact positions. Then if one of you loses visual contact with him, I'll direct another to pick up his trail."

That night, Ingrid's bedroom was an odd combination of frilly feminine things and electronic equipment. On the wall above the communications unit was a large map of the neighborhood. Stuck to it were small, magnetized pieces of metal that could be moved about. They indicated the positions of other agents spotted around in the area, awaiting instructions from Zeke.

"You're sure your sister won't mind our using her room?" he asked Patti.

"Of course not," Patti assured him. "She'll be happy to help the FBI."

Darn Cat, who had been trying without much success to get some sleep, aroused when the cuckoo clock struck nine. He opened his eyes, stretched, and yawned a few times. Finally he stood up.

"Nice kitty, good kitty," Zeke said, by way of encouragement.

"You can save your flattery," Patti told Zeke. "He knows you don't like him."

Zeke picked up the microphone and said into it, "Attention all units. Informant about to leave the house."

D.C. decided he might as well go out; there was too much commotion in the room to sleep, anyway.

"Attention all units," Zeke said into the microphone. "Stand by. Informant about to leave house."

D.C. hid on the other side of a fence until the agents left to look for him, then he crawled out.

Besides he couldn't stand all that sneezing. He crossed the backyard in leisurely fashion. The four agents, hiding in the shadows, watched as he strolled down the alley. He sniffed at a few refuse cans, then vaulted lightly to the top of a fence. He heard a movement behind him and became suspicious, so he jumped down out of sight into a yard.

He waited till Agent Graham had laboriously climbed over, too, then he crawled through a drain-pipe back to the alley again. He came out right at the feet of the other agents who were looking for him.

"We've lost the informant," Agent Webster said into his portable microphone. And they all took off in different directions. When they had left, D. C. continued on his rounds.

Quite some time later, Agent Graham reported to

Zeke, "I've picked him up, on Main Street. He stopped in front of a delicatessen."

"That would be Mr. Meyer's place," Patti told Zeke. "D. C.'s always hanging around there. Drives Mr. Meyer out of his mind."

"Try to keep him in sight," Zeke said into his mike. "Kelly will join you."

Patti and Zeke were standing with their backs to the door and didn't notice when Ingrid walked in. She stopped in her tracks. She looked at the stranger in her room and all the electronic equipment, charts, and other devices, and couldn't believe her eyes.

At last she found her voice. "What on earth goes on here?"

Zeke, without looking around, said sternly, "Quiet, please."

Patti sensed that an explanation was demanded. She said, "Ingrid, I want you to meet Mr. Kelso from the FBI. Mr. Kelso, this is my sister, Ingrid."

But Agent Kelso did not hear. Everything was going wrong. The agent had again lost contact with the informant. (Had they only known, Darn Cat was up in a tree watching *them!*) There was a most distracting conversation going on in the room and he found it difficult to hear his agents in the field.

He was vaguely conscious of a strange voice saying, "Patti, you get Tom Swift and his electric scoreboard out of my room, or I'll call the police," and Patti's reply, "Ingrid, you don't call the police about the FBI."

Zeke would have been even more exasperated if he had had any idea of what was going on right outside the window at that very moment. Mrs. MacDougall was fishing! She had been quite unable to contain her curiosity over the unusual goings on at the Randalls. So, when her husband was dozing, she had snatched his hearing aid and rigged it to a fishing pole. She had then tied the sensitive ear piece to the fish line. If she could just cast it into the bushes under Ingrid's window, she thought, she could hear what that strange man was saying.

"Ka-deep, ka-deep," came over the little receiver. And then she realized it was only a katydid on the window sill.

Snoopy Mrs. MacDougall was determined to listen.

Suddenly, she almost jumped out of her shoes. An arm reached out and grabbed the pole. "I've told you a thousand times," Mr. MacDougall was saying, "to leave my stuff alone." He jerked the pole out of her grasp, untangled the line, and reeled it in. Then he stalked into the house. Mrs. MacDougall followed, very indignant and frustrated.

If her plan had worked, she would have heard Agent Graham's voice as he reported in. "I've got him!"

"Where are you?" Zeke asked excitedly.

"I don't know," came Graham's answer, "and I don't have time to find out! I've doubled back so much...."

Agent Kelly reported in. "I've got him now. He's going into a house, I think. I can see some people through a lighted window."

Zeke tensed. "Move cautiously. They may be armed. And wait for the others," he added.

In a moment of silence, Zeke heard Patti's small voice. "There won't be any shooting, will there?"

"I hope not, Miss Randall," he said gently.

Ingrid, meantime, simply sat down and closed her eyes. "They're all mad," she mumbled. "All mad."

Graham's voice came over. "The front door's unlocked. We're going in!"

"Good," Zeke told him. "But wait for Kelly to cover the back window. Got that, Kelly?"

"Affirmative," came the terse reply.

There were a few moments of stillness, then bedlam broke out in the Randall house. There was the rush of footsteps down the hall, the door to Ingrid's room burst open, and Graham entered, gun leveled. Simultaneously, the window rattled and opened and Agent Kelly stuck his gun in.

"All right, you," he commanded. "Drop it!"

Zeke's gun came out at the first sound. He was so surprised that it was a moment before he recognized his fellow agents. Finally, they all put their weapons away and looked at each other sheepishly.

"The cat came in here," Graham explained.

"Are you out of your mind?" Zeke said. "There's no ca — ca — ." He sneezed violently.

When Patti recovered from her fright, she looked under the bed. The others followed. There was D.C., crouching against the wall.

"The poor darling, he's scared to death," Patti wailed. And Ingrid begged, "Will someone *please* tell me what's going on?"

All Zeke could say, between sneezes, was, "That darn cat!"

That night in the criminals' apartment, Margaret stood in the kitchen and looked hopelessly at the window over the sink. Like all the others, it was nailed down and heavily draped. She didn't know how much longer she would be able to stand the strain.

In a desperate move, she tossed a lighted match

"That darn cat!"

into the wastebasket and held it up to the curtains. The flames leaped high, bringing Dan and Iggy on the run.

Dan quickly put out the fire and turned on Margaret in fury. "Nice try, lady," he said. "Another minute and you'd have had the fire department to the rescue."

Just then there was a knock on the door and the landlady called, "Anybody home?"

Iggy clapped a hand over Margaret's mouth and dragged her to another room. Dan opened the door a crack and the landlady pushed her way in. "Is something on fire?" she asked anxiously.

"It's those awful cigars Iggy smokes," Dan told her.

She wrinkled her nose. "He tells me your mother is sick," she said. "I brought her some hot soup."

Dan took the bowl and thanked her. A moment later, Margaret heard the woman leave. She sank into a chair, weak with despair.

Whenever Mrs. MacDougall wanted a view of the neighborhood, she went out to the front yard and watered the roses. She was at her post the next morning when Gregory Benson drove up to take Ingrid to work.

"I doubt whether Ingrid will feel like going to work today," she told Gregory. "The doctor was in her room till quite late last night."

Gregory showed alarm. Mrs. MacDougall added hastily, "Anyway, I assume he was the doctor."

A few minutes later when Ingrid came out, Gregory greeted her a bit stiffly. "Good morning, Ingrid. I hope you're feeling better today."

Ingrid did not answer. She was in an irritable mood. The night's adventure had upset her, and she was still annoyed at Gregory over the duck incident. When he continued to ask questions, she accused him of listening to Mrs. MacDougall's gossip. Before they had gone three blocks they were quarreling. When Gregory had to stop for a traffic light, Ingrid jumped out of the car in a huff and took a bus to the office.

"I still don't think you can follow a cat night after night," Ingrid said flatly. It was nearly nine o'clock, and Zeke was waiting impatiently for D. C. to stir.

"Supervisor Newton shares your doubts," Zeke

They all looked under the bed and sure enough, there sat Darn Cat, very pleased with himself.

told her. "I had a meeting with him today. He gave me just one more night."

Zeke sneezed. "*Gesundheit,*" Patti said. "Did you tell him about the collar?"

"He took a dim view of that too," Zeke admitted. "He doesn't think you can bug a cat."

"I don't, either," Ingrid said. "Not even Super Cat here."

Zeke put one of two small collars on the growling D. C. Patti picked up the other. "Well, I'm betting on D. C. and the FBI. Here, look." She showed Ingrid one of the studs in the collar. "That is a tiny microphone. Mr. Kelso can hear D. C. meow, and anything that goes on near him. And this," she continued, indicating another tiny stud, "gives off a little beep constantly." She picked up a small portable instrument from among Zeke's gear. "And Mr. Kelso can pick it up on this. It's a direction finder. The needle tells which way D. C.'s going."

"Now I've heard everything," Ingrid remarked skeptically.

"All right, I'll show you," Patti declared. And before the protesting Ingrid quite knew what was happening, Patti gave her the collar and pushed her into a closet in a far part of the house.

"There," she said. "Mr. Kelso will come straight to you. You'll see." And with that she closed the door.

But Agent Kelso did not come right away. Canoe arrived at that moment and Patti left with him for a drive-in movie and forgot to tell Zeke. It soon became stifling in the closet and Ingrid spoke into the tiny collar. It seemed a very silly thing to do.

"Mr. Kelso," she said, "I want out of here."

Zeke, who was absorbed in his plans for the night, was startled at the sound of a voice. Absent-mindedly, he turned to D. C. and said, "It isn't nine o'clock yet, old man."

Ingrid discovered to her horror that the latch was stuck and she was trapped inside the closet. She pounded on the door and screamed. Finally Zeke heard. He grabbed the direction finder and went straight to the rescue.

He pulled on the knob with all his strength, but

The latch stuck and Ingrid almost smothered before Zeke rescued her.

the latch held. There was nothing to do but remove the hinges. Then, as Ingrid pushed, he gave a mighty jerk, and the door flew off. He fell backwards on the floor, the door came down on top of him, and Ingrid, exhausted and disheveled, and very, very angry, landed atop the heap.

When Zeke got back to the bedroom, D. C. had left. Quickly he collected his instruments but when he got to the alley, the signals from D. C.'s collar were very faint. He ran as fast as he could in the direction indicated, and finally caught up with his informant. He was sitting atop a fence, enjoying the frenzied barking of a dog on the ground below. Zeke, though, did not enjoy it. The sound coming through the receiver almost split his eardrums.

Finally D. C. tired of the dog's noise, and jumped down on the other side of the fence. He found himself in a drive-in movie. Soon he realized that the area was truly a gold mine of discarded bits of food. While D. C. walked happily under the cars, Zeke was having his troubles.

"Hey, mister," the manager shouted at him. "You can't drive in there without a car!"

Zeke was too busy trailing Darn Cat to explain, so the manager gave chase. Zeke's instruments told him that he was right upon his informant, but he could not see hide or hair of him. Then it occurred to him that D. C. might be in a car. Sure enough,

D.C. almost tripped a man juggling two large trays of French fries, hot dogs, and malted milks.

there sat Canoe and Patti in a car nearby, unaware that D. C. was in the back seat.

Agent Kelso from that moment was a very busy man. He had to get D. C. back on the job again, and he had to elude the manager. He simply didn't have time to explain that he was an FBI agent trailing a cat.

By tossing tiny pebbles at the car, he eventually attracted Patti's attention and got her to put D. C. out of the car. Then the chase really got under way. D. C., sensing that something was wrong, ran for his life. He darted around and over parked cars, up one row and down another. Zeke managed to keep him in sight. Meantime, the manager was determined to capture this madman who was disturbing his customers. In the emergency, he took to the tops of the cars where he could make better speed, frightening the occupants almost out of their wits.

At last Darn Cat saw an unobstructed path ahead of him and darted down it. It was the path to the refreshment stand and a portly man had just started down it, *en route* to his family car. He carried a cardboard tray full of malted milks, hot dogs, and French fries.

When he saw a large cat almost under his feet he did a neat balancing act. He twisted and turned in the manner of a ballet dancer and managed to miss D. C. Hot on his heels came Zeke, but luckily they managed to dodge each other. The man sighed with relief and took a few steps forward. This time he was off guard. He and the manager collided head on. Both went crashing down in a messy avalanche of French fries, hot dogs, and malted milks.

For Zeke it was a fortunate accident. He was able to follow the informant without further incident back to the Randall neighborhood. D. C. decided to drop by and annoy Blitzy before turning in. In Gregory's backyard, he swatted at the pigeon cage, arousing all the birds, then headed for the back door. Blitzy barked hysterically. The noises brought Gregory to the kitchen window with a shotgun. He didn't see D. C., but he thought he could make out a man's form in the shrubbery. He fired a shot into the air. D. C. shot out of there as though jet-

The irate manager was covered with ice cream and mustard from head to toe.

propelled. Then Gregory thought he saw a man darting across the yard, so he fired a second blast and gave chase.

Moments before, Canoe had brought Patti home from the drive-in movie, and was just returning to his car when he heard the shots. As he stood listening, the action started. First, D. C. shot by him, then came Zeke full steam ahead. Next thing he knew, a man was running toward him, wildly brandishing a shotgun. Canoe had no wish to be a dead hero. He immediately raised both hands in surrender.

But Gregory charged past him and up the Randall steps. Gun in hand, he alternately rang the bell, pounded on the door, and shouted, creating a great uproar.

Upstairs in the temporary communications center there was near panic. Patti was wringing her hands and crying, "They've shot D. C., I know they have."

"D. C.'s all right," Zeke consoled her. "They missed him by a mile." As the hammering continued, he started pulling out his equipment in alarm.

"It's Gregory," Ingrid whispered. "He belonged to the duck D. C. stole. He gets awful mad awful fast."

"You'd better let him in," he told Ingrid. "But whatever else you do, keep him out of this room."

While Ingrid went to the door, Patti and Zeke

grabbed wildly at everything that was not Ingrid's and tossed it into the clothes closet.

"If you came here to murder D. C. in cold blood — " they heard Ingrid saying. And Gregory retorted, "I'm not after your stupid cat. I saw a prowler head this way. I've got to search your house — make sure you're safe."

Zeke grabbed the last bit of evidence and jumped into the closet only seconds before Gregory entered the bedroom. Afterwards he never could explain it, but just as he was closing the closet door, D. C. shot in too.

D. C. rubbed against Zeke's legs and he felt a sneeze coming on. He pressed a forefinger tightly against the base of his nose to suppress it. He knew he couldn't hold out very long. He was smothering in the clothing and equipment and he scarcely had room to breathe.

He sighed with relief as Gregory appeared to be leaving. Then it happened. D. C. began howling. Zeke was paralyzed by shock as D. C. continued shrieking as only a Siamese can. It belatedly dawned upon Zeke that he was standing on D. C.'s tail.

He raised a foot, and D.C. shot out as the door was flung open. Zeke and Gregory stood nose to nose, staring at each other. Gregory stood glued to the floor, holding his shotgun by the barrel.

Zeke was the first to recover. "The wiring seems

to be okay, Miss Randall," he said as nonchalantly as he could. He got out of the house before the dumbfounded Gregory could stop him.

Supervisor Newton would have closed the books on Darn Cat Randall, informant, had it not been for Patti. Zeke had used up his last chance the night before. Patti, though, was sure that if they would only be patient, D.C. would lead them to Miss Miller.

After Ingrid left for work the next morning, Patti made a call at the jewelry store of her good friend, Mr. Hofstedder. Mr. Hofstedder was a very elderly and very honorable man. When Patti outlined the plan her fertile little brain had devised, he clapped his hands over his face in despair. But eventually she won him over.

She telephoned the FBI, and asked for Supervisor Newton. "I am Miss Daphne Hofstedder," she told him, disguising her voice, "and I have some information. About two weeks ago, I sold a watchband to Miss Margaret Miller, the one who was kidnapped by the bank robbers." Patti described the expansion bracelet and the watch to an excited Mr. Newton. She added that she had been out of town and had only just heard of the kidnapping.

When she hung up, the supervisor turned to Zeke. "Well, there's no question about what the cat dragged in, to coin a phrase. It is Margaret Miller's watch. I think we'd better pursue the cat angle a bit further. In my twenty-five years with the Bureau," Newton added, "this is the craziest lead I've ever heard of."

As luck (or possibly feline contrariness) would have it, Darn Cat overslept that night. Supervisor Newton himself took charge of the surveillance, operating the main communications control in Ingrid's room. This was so that Zeke could direct the actual trailing of D.C.

Mr. Newton kept looking at his watch, and suggested they give the slumbering informant a tiny shove. Patti explained that this would be the worst possible psychology.

"When I think of that poor little helpless cat walking into that bunch of desperate criminals," she said, "I can hardly stand it."

"That cat is about as helpless as the U.S. Marine Corps," Ingrid remarked. But she was worried too.

When D. C. awoke and stretched, Supervisor Newton spoke into the communications panel. "Attention all units. Informant about to leave. You will monitor Agent Kelso's movements. Take no action until you get word from me. Out."

Zeke was heavily armed and carried his miniature sending and receiving set and the direction finder. He watched as D. C. sauntered across the backyard

D.C. was so hungry he did not realize he was being followed by a whole procession of people.

toward the alley where two agents picked him up. A half dozen agents were spotted around the neighborhood on foot, and two Bureau cars were alert and standing by.

Patti nervously watched him from Ingrid's room. "He's down by the trash barrel playing it cool," she told Mr. Newton.

"What's the matter with him?" the supervisor wanted to know. "Why doesn't he move?"

Patti shook her head. "You need someone down there who understands cats, Mr. Newton," she said. "Especially D. C. Now if you'd let me go along..."

"You'll just have to leave it up to the FBI, Miss Randall," he told her. "We take excellent care of our men and our informants."

Patti nodded. Supervisor Newton was relieved

when she quietly left. Now he could give his full attention to directing the surveillance. She went through the darkened house to the kitchen, arriving just in time to see Zeke head for the alley.

If Darn Cat had had the slightest idea of the procession he was leading, he probably would have dreamed up some clever trap. But he was hungry, practically starving, in fact, and he remembered where he had had some divine food. So he was not as cautious as he usually was.

He didn't realize that "that man" was following his every movement. Neither did Zeke realize that Patti was following him. And Patti never dreamed that Canoe was following her. As it happened, Canoe had driven up just in time to see Patti shadowing a strange man across the backyard. And since she had been acting a bit peculiarly lately, he decided to trail her.

And these weren't all. Mrs. MacDougall's curiosity had reached the explosion stage. She had heard voices in the night, and seen strange men about the Randall house. When she saw Zeke dart across the backyard, she put a scarf over her head and tiptoed to the door, hoping Mr. MacDougall wouldn't notice.

He did, however, and held his foot against the door. "Where do you think you're going?" he asked nastily.

"There's something fishy going on around here," she replied, "and I intend to find out what it is." She pushed him aside and left.

Mr. MacDougall, whistling softly to himself, went to the phone and dialed a number. A moment later, he said, "Police? I want to report a prowler — a man, dressed like an old woman....Yes....Yes, I've seen him before. I think he may be dangerous." Then he hung up, removed his hearing aid, and went happily to bed.

Mrs. MacDougall, of course, got a late start and when she reached the alley, no one was in sight. Actually, D. C. was in the next block. Zeke watched him walk along on a rather high fence, then disappear on the other side. Zeke, who had to keep in form at all times, leaped nimbly over a few moments later. D. C. led him a hazardous course through backyards filled with many obstacles, such as bicycles, refuse cans, flower beds and the like. But Zeke was able to follow, aided by his direction finder and the 'beep-beep' broadcast from the cat's collar.

Patti had a much harder time, but Zeke was a much larger object to trail than D. C., and she managed to keep him in sight. Canoe, on the other hand, ran into trouble. He had never been noted for caution, and he leaped over the fence without first looking on the other side. He alighted square on a trampoline. The taut canvas was a perfect landing

Never noted for caution, Canoe didn't look on the other side of the fence, and got a big surprise.

pad. Canoe flew through the air, and landed twenty feet away in a swimming pool.

While all this was going on, Mrs. MacDougall was looking in vain for the action, and the police were looking for Mrs. MacDougall. She went scampering down the alley, stopped to listen, peered over a fence and into a nearby lighted window. Seeing nothing, she turned suddenly to reverse her direction and ran smack into the arms of a tall policeman.

A second policeman materialized, and when she saw his gun, she stifled a scream. "Don't bother to put on an act," the first policeman said, pushing her away. "We know who you are."

Mrs. MacDougall, when she had recovered from shock, was furious. The policeman with the gun tried to search her, and she slapped him soundly. "How dare you?" she said angrily.

The officers pinned her arms down, although they

met with considerable resistance. As they led her off to the police car, one of them told her, "I don't want to tell you how to run your racket, Mac, but if I were you I wouldn't wear women's clothes. With *your* face, you can't get by with it."

Darn Cat was thinking that if he remembered correctly (and he always did), he was almost at that new place where they had given him the salmon. He paused to make sure and to listen. He heard a peculiar "squish, squish" sound some distance behind him and wondered what it was. Zeke heard it, and wondered too. And Patti, trailing Zeke, had to stop also, and hide behind some bushes. Then *she* heard it — "squish, squish."

The sound was made by Canoe's soaking wet shoes on the alley pavement. When the procession, led by D. C., started moving again, it was in Canoe's direction. He flattened himself against an overhead garage door.

And then a most amazing thing happened. A light went on in the garage, there was a small clicking noise, and suddenly the door went up, taking Canoe with it. Unsuspectingly, a woman drove her car out and away. Only poor Canoe's sodden feet could be seen sticking out from under the garage roof. He found himself in a trap quite beyond his power to spring.

Of the four people who originally were trailing D. C., only two were left. Zeke watched breathlessly as the informant crossed a yard between two apartment houses and started up the steps. Patti's heart almost stopped beating. Quickly, Zeke got the address of the building and reported it to Supervisor Newton back at the communications control. He ordered all agents to converge on the site.

D. C. sat at the back door, wondering if he would be able to arouse anyone's attention. Then he had a stroke of luck. The man called Iggy was coming up the stairs, and when he let himself in, D. C. shot in too.

"I got a laundry truck," he told Dan. "Just the thing for this job. No one can see in."

Dan nodded. "You get her," he said, indicating Margaret. "I'll handle the money. The sooner we clear out of here the better."

No one noticed D. C., so he meowed to attract their attention. Iggy was surprised and pleased. He bent down and picked the cat up. "You just wait a minute, old buddy," he said to D. C. "I've got some business to attend to. Then I'll give you a nice piece of fish."

Zeke clearly heard Iggy's words, broadcast by the tiny transmitter on D. C.'s collar. There followed a snarl from D. C. and the faint background scream of a woman. Then came Dan's angry voice, "The cat's bugged — ," and the sound went dead.

Iggy bent down and picked up D.C. A moment later Zeke heard
Dan's voice say, "The cat's bugged!"

Zeke thought fast. This was the worst thing that could have happened. Now the criminals knew they were being watched. He couldn't wait for the others to join him as he had been instructed. He so advised Main Control, then stepped to the door where he had seen D. C. and the man enter.

The door inched open in answer to his knock, and Dan looked out suspiciously. Zeke smiled pleasantly. "Sorry to bother you, but I've lost my cat," he said. "I thought he might have strayed in here."

Dan studied him in silence. Zeke continued, "Do you mind if I look?"

Dan opened the door wider. "Come right in."

Zeke stepped in cautiously. His eyes swept the empty kitchen and traveled to the living room beyond. "Why, there he is on the mantel," he said, pointing to the growling, hostile D.C. "Mind if I get him?" Zeke went into the next room, and Dan followed close behind, his hands on his gun.

"Hi, old man," Zeke said to D. C., hoping against hope that his informant would let bygones be bygones. "Am I glad to see you!" He reached out a hand to grab D. C. and at the same time sneezed violently. D. C. lashed out furiously, but Zeke was prepared and eluded the claws.

"I don't think he likes you much," Dan observed.

"Well, to be honest, we barely tolerate each other," Zeke admitted. "Actually, he's my wife's cat."

Out of the corner of his eye, Zeke saw a man emerge from the bedroom. He pretended not to notice that the two of them were steadily closing in on him. He had a plan, if he could just get hold of D. C., and if he could stop sneezing, and if his eyes didn't swell shut.

"My wife goes wild when he strays away," Zeke chattered, playing for time. "Sometimes I think she loves him more than she does me...."

He was interrupted by a knock at the door. Dan, standing behind Zeke, took his gun out, then nodded to Iggy to open the door. Zeke's heart sank. In came Patti.

"Oh, there you are," she said to Zeke, as happily

"You'd better let me handle this, dear," Zeke said, play-acting, but he didn't fool the criminals.

unconcerned as though she were at a friend's house. "You found him!"

She pushed past Iggy, who didn't quite know what to do, and gathered the willing D. C. in her arms. "We've been so worried about you, darling," she cooed.

"I'd rather you let me handle this, dear," Zeke told her, play-acting, though he was quite sure they weren't fooling the criminals. He wondered if any of them, including Margaret Miller, would get out of there alive. He could only pray for a miracle. He didn't dare make a move to apprehend the criminals with Patti in the room.

Patti backed toward the door. "Why don't we all go, now that we've found D. C." She took Zeke's arm cozily.

Dan, who had remained partially hidden from her view, stepped out, his gun in Zeke's side. "Let's stop playing games," he snapped. "Iggy, get the money together. We're cutting out."

Iggy nodded toward the bedroom. "What about her?"

"Forget her. We'll take Little Miss Nosey here," he answered, referring to Patti. He turned to Zeke. "All right, Copper, hands on top of your head."

Patti, terrified, didn't know what to do. She released Zeke's arm in order to hold the squirming frightened D. C. Suddenly, with muscles of steel,

Iggy started cramming bills into the suitcase, but Patti leaped at him and fought like a tiger.

Darn Cat sprang out of her arms and landed in the face of the astonished Dan. Zeke, in one lightning movement, delivered a right to the criminal's jaw and knocked the gun from his hand. They both went to the floor, fighting furiously for possession of the weapon.

Iggy, leaving Dan to take care of himself, started cramming bills into the suitcase, preparatory to flight. But Patti leaped on his back and fought like a tigress. Every time he got the suitcase almost fastened, she managed to kick it open, scattering the money.

Meantime, D. C. jumped back up onto the mantel and viewed the feverish activity with little concern. He couldn't help his girl, and that man that sneezed, well, he couldn't care less what happened to him. In fact, he wondered why he was wasting time there at all. The back door was ajar, he noticed, so he wandered out on the landing. He was sitting there, minding his own business and trying to decide where to go to next, when the door flew back with a bang and the fish man came out with the suitcase.

D. C. tried to get out of his way but only succeeded in tripping him. Iggy lost his balance and fell down the stairs, and the money came tumbling after. When he hit the bottom, the packages of money were all about him. He stretched out both hands to recover them and a pair of handcuffs appeared out of nowhere and clamped about his wrists.

The other agents, guided by Supervisor Newton, had arrived in the nick to time. Zeke had just delivered Dan a knockout blow, partially powered by a forceful sneeze. Patti had found Margaret Miller in the bedroom. She was gagged and bound but unharmed.

The next day the newspapers played up the story to its full extent. D. C. stared out from the front page of every edition. The headline writers had enjoyed themselves immensely. UNDERCOVER CAT ROUNDS UP KILLERS. DARN CAT GETS HIS MAN. FBI LAUDS FEARLESS FELINE. And under one picture D. C. was quoted as saying, "It was nothing. It was only what any patriotic American cat would have done."

Patti showed D. C. his pictures but he couldn't have cared less. "I'll bet you'll get a Congressional medal or something," she told him.

"Look," cried Ingrid. "See how your boyfriend spends his nights." She pointed to a large photo on the second page.

Patti grabbed it and read the caption aloud, "'Youth trapped in garage door. Freed by fire department after eight-hour ordeal.' Now how do you suppose he did that?"

The morning newspapers quoted D.C.: "It was only what any patriotic American cat would have done."

The doorbell sounded, and Ingrid, dressed for work, said, "That won't be Gregory. Not after last night." It was, though, and he was all smiles and forgiveness.

"Good morning, good morning," he said brightly. And seeing Patti holding D. C. in her arms, he added, "Good morning, Patricia. How's our little celebrity this morning?"

He tried to chuck D. C. under the chin, but Darn Cat knew a hypocrite when he saw one. He snarled and lashed out a paw with claws bared.

Ingrid smiled as she saw Zeke drive up and park his car behind Gregory's. A little pixie whispered in her ear. She allowed Gregory to follow her out to the curb, talking all kinds of silly nonsense in order to make amends. She paused beside Zeke's car, however, and Gregory absent-mindedly held the door open for her.

Zeke grinned. "Thank you, old man," he said, and drove off with the delighted Ingrid before Gregory quite realized what he had done.

Patti was still standing on the front steps holding D. C. when Canoe drove up. He did not hop out lightly as was his custom. Instead he walked stiffly and his head was turned slightly to one side as though it had not been put on straight.

Patti regarded him with sympathy. "You poor dear. Was it awful, up there on the garage door all night?"

He nodded. "Canoe, how on earth did you do it?"

"Well, you see," he began, "you were acting so strangely — why didn't you tell me?"

"The FBI. They wouldn't let me tell anyone."

"I was so worried about you," he explained. "And I came over last night and I saw you following a man...."

Patti's eyes brimmed. "Oh, Canoe! You were jealous?"

He nodded. She put D. C. down and took Canoe by the arm. "Come on in the house and build yourself a weird sandwich and tell me all about it."

D. C. watched his girl go in the house with her young man. How he loved that girl. The whole Randall family, for that matter. And he liked that character who was always hanging around eating tasty sandwiches. He hoped, however, that that man who sneezed would not become a permanent guest. He disliked him almost as much as he did Blitzy's human. Almost, but not quite.

This hero stuff is very hard on the nerves, D.C. thought, as he wandered off to get some sleep.